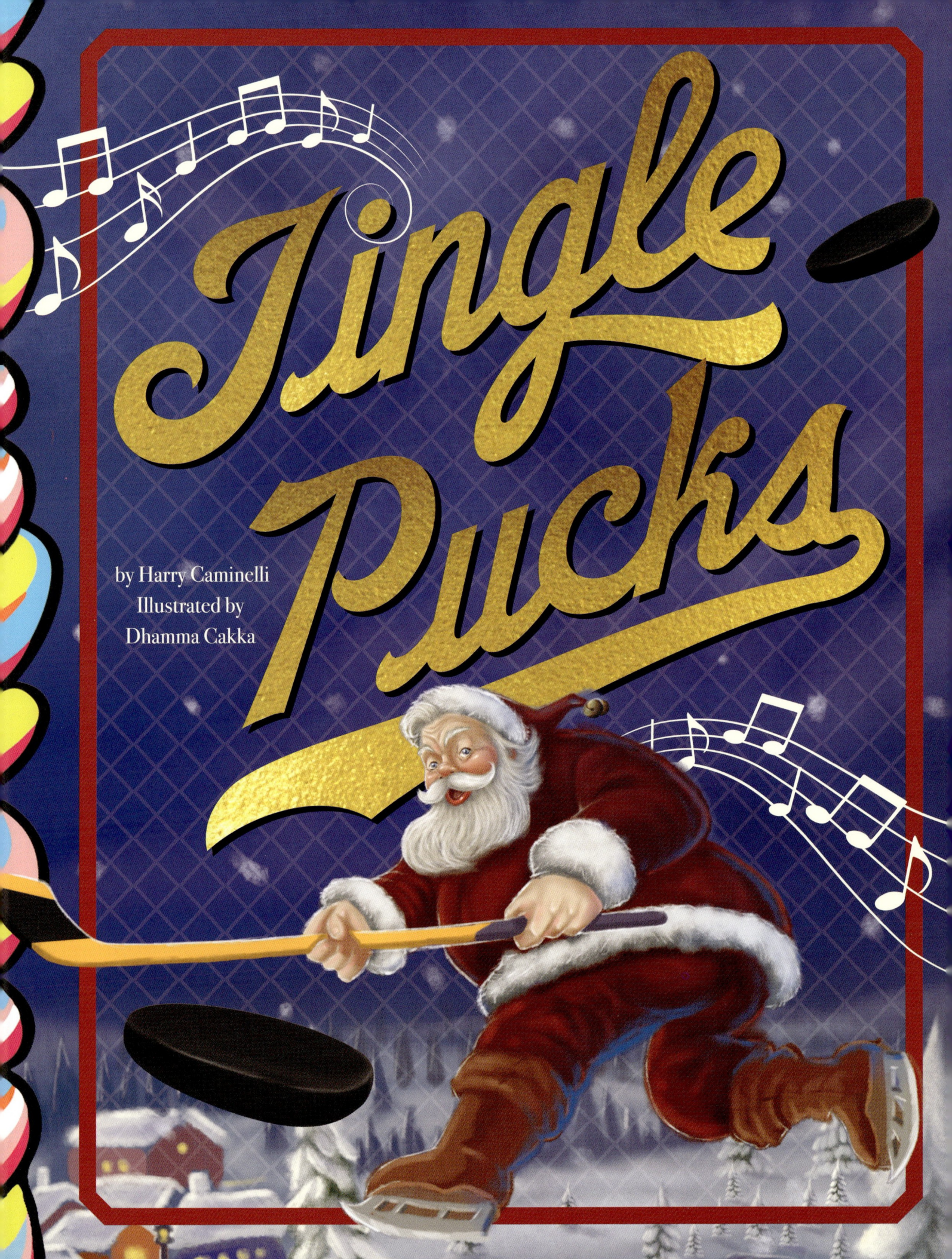

Dashing down the ice
on a partial breakaway,
splittin' the D he'll go,
laughing all the way!
Ha-Ha-Ha!

The fans he likes to please,
so he'll place the shot just right.
What fun it is to go top cheese!
Let's win this game tonight!

Oh! Jingle pucks, jingle pucks,
jingle all the way!
Oh, what fun it is to score
and hear the music play! Hey!
Jingle pucks, jingle pucks,
jingle all the way!
Oh, what fun it is to score
and hear the music play! Hey!

A long, long time ago,
some elves made quite a find.
Out there amidst the ice and snow
a star was left behind.

Mis emociones
son un mar de colores
que suben y bajan
y cambian sin parar.
Todas ellas son parte de mí
y sus colores me hacen
ser quien soy.

And as the story goes,
he was found at center ice.
How he got there, no one knows,
but his shot was really nice!

Oh! Jingle pucks, jingle pucks,
jingle all the way!
Oh, what fun it is to score
and hear the music play! Hey!
Jingle pucks, jingle pucks,
jingle all the way!
Oh, what fun it is to score
and hear the music play! Hey!

The guy could really skate.
Hockey Santa was his name.
His training made him great.
He worked all aspects of his game.

The elves all coached him up.

He was the best they'd ever met.

When he played you'd hear them say,

"He's got a great nose for the net!"

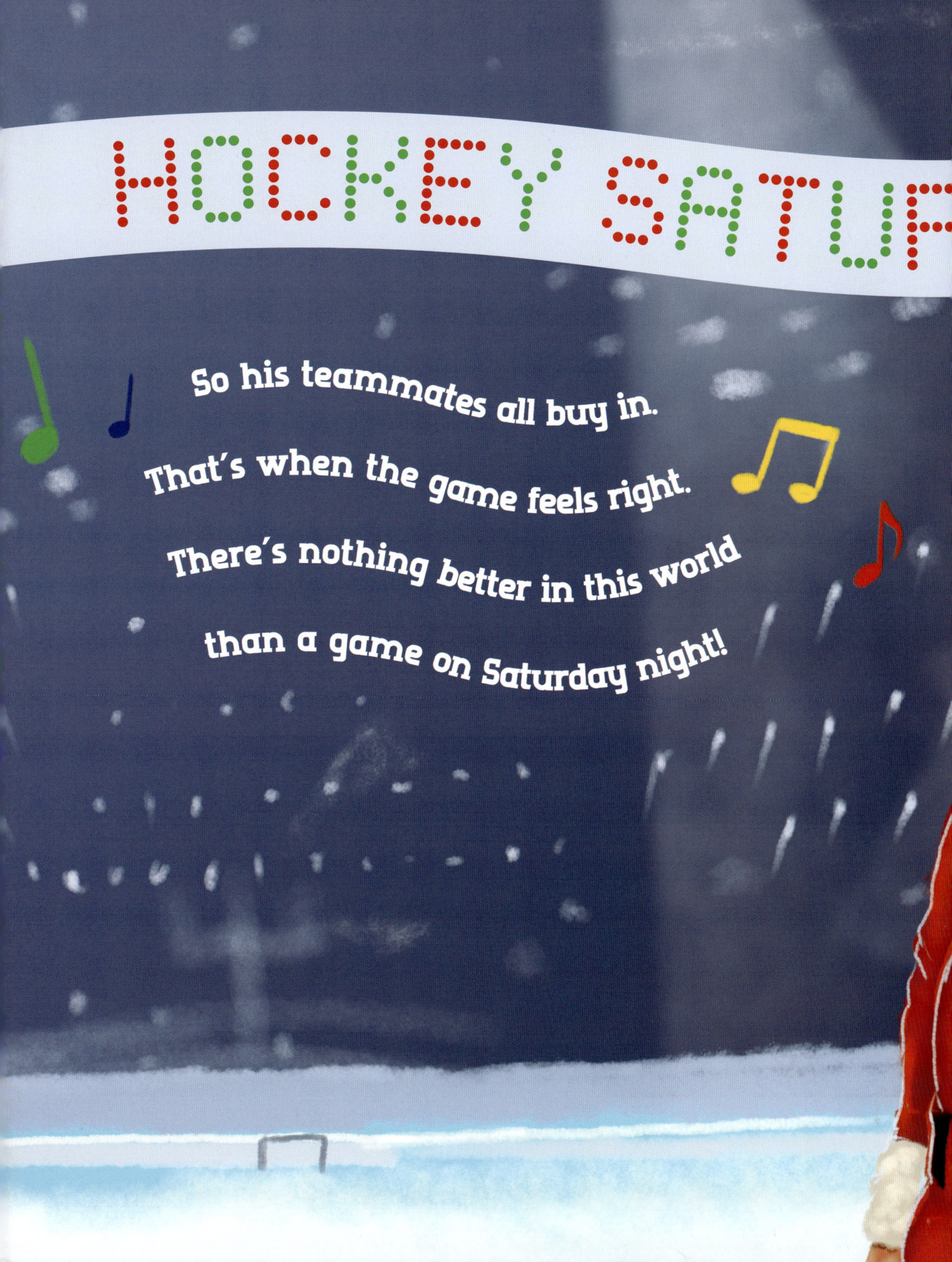

HOCKEY SATU[RDAY]

So his teammates all buy in.
That's when the game feels right.
There's nothing better in this world
than a game on Saturday night!